Dip Into A Story

Volume 1

Dip Into A Story

Volume 1

Large Print Edition

Cathy Emma Laybourn

Contents

These stories are also published in
the ebook by Cathy Emma Laybourn:
Coffee-break Stories and Tea-time Tales
1st Collection:
Twenty Magazine Short Stories

The stories were originally published
In various magazines:
Take a Break
Take a Break Fiction Feast
The People's Friend
That's Life (Australia)

Remember You're a Star

'Come on, Zoe!' Tom muttered. 'Where are you? I'm starving!' He checked his watch. How long did it take to fetch a Chinese takeaway?

It was his turn to cook, but after a hard day at the office he really didn't feel up to it. Zoe's job wasn't nearly as exhausting as his, he thought resentfully. There was no need for her to have looked so weary when he asked her to go out for a sweet and sour.

And she was taking her time! She was supposed to ring when she was setting off back home. So where was she?

Impatiently Tom got his mobile out and keyed her number – only to hear the familiar ringtone a few yards away in the hall. The stupid girl! Where had she left her mobile?

Tom found it in the pocket of her other coat. He was about to lay it prominently on the hall table to make her feel guilty, when it bleeped to say a text had just come through.

Idly, Tom pressed READ. Not that he was prying, but what was Zoe's was his too, right? Anyway, it wasn't as if she had any secrets.

Or that was what he'd assumed. So he stared at the text with incredulity.

Zoe love Remember you're a star

Zoe? A star? Who'd sent this message to his wife? Tom was perplexed for a moment, until he laughed out loud.

Of course! It'd be her mum. Or perhaps her sister, or one of those dizzy girl-friends of hers. Strangely, though, it hadn't come up with a sender's name, just a number.

He wasn't sure if it was a familiar one or not: all mobile numbers looked so alike.

Tom hesitated for a moment. Then he scrolled through the contact list on Zoe's phone. That number wasn't her mum's, or her sister's; it wasn't listed there at all. That was odd.

He knew he should have put the phone down then. Instead, as if his fingers had taken on a life of their own, he found himself looking up past text messages.

They were mostly from him, saying he'd be home late or don't forget to buy milk; but scattered amongst them, more texts from that strange number reappeared. And not just once.

Hey Zoe U R unique and wonderful!

And then again: **You are an amazing person, don't forget that**

And finally: **No matter what Tom says, you are not stupid!! U R talented and kind and so much more**

He froze, staring at the screen. No matter what Tom says? Who had she been talking to about him? And when had he called her stupid?

Well, five minutes ago, for a start... and also yesterday, when she'd left the iron on and scorched his shirt collar after he'd asked her to make a cup of tea.

Or hang on, maybe it was a few days ago when she'd filled the car up at the expensive petrol station instead of at the cheaper one. Or that time last week when he thought she'd forgotten the dry cleaning, even though she hadn't...

4

Tom felt uncomfortable. He'd been pretty annoyed on each occasion. Calling Zoe stupid had just been a way of letting off steam. It wasn't as if he'd really meant it.

But to a stranger, who didn't know the circumstances, it might not seem that reasonable.

A stranger? he thought grumpily.
Some stranger – calling my wife a star!
No stranger to Zoe, that was for sure!

He jumped at the scrape of a key in the lock. There was just enough time to slip the phone back into Zoe's coat pocket before she came in.

'Sorry I was so long,' said Zoe anxiously. 'There was a massive queue at the takeaway.'

'Don't worry about it! Come on, let's eat it while it's hot.'

Tom hurried her into the kitchen, not wanting her to check her phone right now. But he was hunting for clues. So once they sat down to eat, he asked casually, 'Good day at work?'

'Not really,' Zoe said.

'How's that?'

'Oh, they've just reorganised our client list again. You wouldn't be interested.'

'Yes, I would,' said Tom, although normally at this point he would launch into a detailed account of his own day. 'What's the problem?'

It took some coaxing out of her: she was so sure that she must be boring him. But Tom listened attentively, wondering about that anonymous texter as he noted the names of her colleagues. They'd never really registered with him before.

Neither had the complexity of Zoe's job. He'd assumed that co-ordinating care for the elderly must be a doddle, and he was taken aback at the size of her client list. All that red tape to negotiate...

'Can't you get an assistant?' he asked.

'Oh, yes!' She smiled. 'We've got a new lad, Lucas, but he's only temporary and he's not trained up yet.'

'Not much use, then?'

'Oh, he's clever enough. Incredibly good-looking, too. Mike says he'll turn the old ladies' heads if we ever let him loose on the home visits!'

Zoe laughed, and Tom realised that this was the most animated he had seen her in days. Was it his imagination, or had she brightened up at the mere mention of Lucas?

That was a definite suspect. After all, where else was she going to meet a stranger who might call her a star?

Another answer came all too readily. Zoe went out running twice a week. Tom had never bothered going with her – but now he began to put feelers out about her route.

'Twice round the park is usually enough,' said Zoe. 'Why do you ask?'

'Oh – I want to make sure you're safe, that's all,' said Tom, patting her shoulder. 'You might meet some strange characters in the park.'

She shrugged. 'Only other runners, and a few dog walkers!'

'Maybe I'll join you one of these days,' said Tom. Zoe looked surprised. After a moment's hesitation she answered.

'Well, sure. That would be great!'

That evening, Tom couldn't help noticing that Zoe seemed unusually relaxed and cheerful. So who had put her in such a good mood?

Was it the same person who had sent those texts? They might be perfectly innocent – but he couldn't ask without betraying the uncomfortable fact that he had been prying on Zoe's phone.

So for the next few days, Tom simply watched and waited; and whenever he got the chance, although he knew it was an underhand thing to do, he checked her phone for messages.

Zoe stay strong you're a special person

On reading that, Tom ground his teeth. Then he rang the strange number from his own phone, his heart pounding anxiously as he mentally rehearsed what he might say.

The line was dead. Not even a message function. It must be switched off, or have no signal...

On Sunday, Tom went running in the park with Zoe, closely watching everyone they met.

It wasn't a successful outing. The runners and dog-walkers included several young men and women who seemed to recognise Zoe, but they gave her no more than casual greetings. There were no obvious clues.

Moreover, Tom, to his dismay, realised that he wasn't as fit as he'd assumed. He could barely keep up with his wife. It was humiliating to puff along behind her, and be overtaken by fitter and speedier young men.

By the time they got home he was breathless and bad-tempered.

His mood wasn't improved when he sneaked a look at Zoe's phone while she was in the shower and saw the text, which had arrived just ten minutes previously:

Zoe never mind him. You know you are a lovely, lovable girl

Tom felt a surge of anger, mixed with a strange panic. What was going on? Lovable – well, sure – but who was telling her so?

Was it one of those runners after all, who'd spotted him shouting at Zoe to slow down? Or who had passed them as he was snapping at her on the way home?

He hadn't meant to snap. It had only been because he was so hot and tired. But now he didn't know what to think. Where was this secret stranger? Park or work – or somewhere else again?

The question was obsessing him. He began to ask Zoe about her work every evening over tea.

She looked at him curiously. 'You never used to take an interest, Tom!'

'I never realised exactly what you did,' he said. 'I'm interested now. So did you take the handsome Lucas on any home visits yet, to stun the old ladies?'

'Not yet. Mike says he's too young.'

'Too young?'

'Well, he's only seventeen! He's back in college next month. But I think the work experience has done him good: Mike's been impressed with him.'

Tom struck Lucas off his suspect list, and began to wonder about Mike instead.

'Is Mike impressed with you?'

'I certainly hope so! It was him who put me in for the promotion.'

'Nice guy, is he?'

'He's great,' said Zoe. 'He's so kind and helpful. He always listens, and he really knows his stuff.' She was smiling again.

But Tom was depressed. He remembered that Mike's name had been mentioned the other day, when she had been so animated.

Now the same thing had happened again. As she described how supportive this wonderful Mike was, she looked happy – even glowing.

Mike was a sympathetic boss. He'd probably encouraged her to spill out all the marital secrets: he'd listened all right, as Zoe told him all her husband's slights and put-downs.

Because Mike would never treat her that way, thought Tom bitterly. Mike thought she was wonderful. Mike thought she was a star.

Tom got up from the table abruptly and began to crash plates into the dishwasher.

'Tom? Are you annoyed at something?' said Zoe hesitantly.

'Don't be stupid,' he said shortly. But of course he was annoyed. He barely spoke to her for the next hour, until his mate Lee rang. Then he slammed out in a sullen temper to meet Lee and watch the football at the pub.

When he got in, it was late, and Zoe was already in bed. He couldn't resist. He fished her phone out of her bag and checked it. And there was that number again.

Don't let Tom get you down. You are extraordinary and don't you forget it!

So Zoe had already been complaining about his behaviour to the mystery messager.

Though Tom had to admit that she had something to complain about... There had been no good reason for him to stamp out in a sulk and leave her alone all evening. He knew that in his heart.

Tom spent a largely sleepless night. He tossed and turned and brooded about Mike, who was probably just as good-looking as Lucas, but with added experience...

And who was kind, and thought his wife was wonderful. Tom listened to Zoe's gentle breathing in the bed beside him, and remembered the way her face had lit up at Mike's name. Well, naturally she would prefer the company of someone who called her a star to a husband who called her stupid.

He shouldn't have said that.

She hadn't deserved that. Zoe **was** a star –
he wouldn't have married her otherwise.
She was amazing and extraordinary. But now
Tom found himself wondering if **he** was
amazing and extraordinary enough for **her**.

He rolled over, fretting. What if he had
turned her away, into Mike's arms? What
if she decided she would rather be with
someone kinder?

Tom didn't think he was an unkind person.
But somehow his more generous side was
seldom uppermost. Even his mate Lee had
labelled him a grumpy so-and-so this
evening…

Tom felt dimly that perhaps he could try
harder to be nice – the way Zoe tried to be
nice to him. No matter how he searched his
memory, he couldn't remember that she'd
ever called him stupid, or any other
contemptuous name.

But certain things that he had said to Zoe echoed through his head. How many times had he ignored her, or shut her down? And if she'd objected, he'd just gone into a sulk...

It was a long time before he slept.

In the morning Zoe brought him a cup of tea, with no recriminations for his late night or his bad temper.

'Sorry I snapped last night,' he muttered, and saw shock in Zoe's face.

Shock? Just because he'd apologised? But then it was a long time since he'd apologised for anything.

'Good match?' she said coolly.

'Yeah, not bad. I'd rather have been at home with you.'

'That was your choice,' she said quietly, and began to pull clothes from the wardrobe.

A week ago he would have retorted something sharp. Now he watched her with a new insecurity. Zoe had someone else to call her wonderful: she didn't need a grouchy husband. He made an effort.
'Have you got a busy day today?' he asked.

'Reviewing cases with Mike,' she answered briefly, and turned her back on him.

No wonder she was in such a hurry, he thought dismally. She couldn't wait to get to work...

The panic rose in his throat again. What if Zoe decided she was fed up? What if she turned her back on him for good? He wanted to say something warm and loving to her, but he couldn't think of the right words. Before he managed to say anything, she had left.

That evening Tom got home early. Although it wasn't his turn, he began to prepare tea. Pasta with salmon in a creamy sauce: something a bit special. He'd been shopping in his lunch hour to make sure he had the ingredients.

A bottle of white wine went into the fridge. Then he waited for Zoe to come home.

She was late. He began to feel afraid; and when he finally heard her key, he hurried to open the door.

'Sorry! There was an emergency with an old lady, and we ended up working overtime,' said Zoe. 'I missed the train, so Mike gave me a lift.' She turned to smile and wave at the car that was just pulling away.

'That's Mike?' Tom gazed at the departing car, but only caught a glimpse of greying hair. So maybe Mike was just a father figure...

Or maybe not. Either way, it hurt to think that Zoe might have turned to Mike for comfort instead of to her husband.

Zoe pulled her coat off, looking weary. 'I know it's my turn to cook,' she said, 'but how do you feel about a takeaway?'

'No need. Tea's all ready.'

Her eyes widened. 'Really? How come?'

'I thought you deserved a break,' he said. 'You work hard. I just wanted to say, I think you're brilliant.' It came out awkwardly.

She studied him with a tiny frown. 'Tom? Has something happened? You haven't crashed the car, have you?'

He tried to laugh. 'Can't I pay you a compliment without you asking why?'

'You don't do compliments, that's all.'

Her phone bleeped, and as she pulled it from her bag, Tom's heart began to ache. Mike had only just driven away, and he was texting her already!

He forced himself to ask. 'Anything important?'

'It's from Mum. She says, don't forget your Gran's birthday – as if I would! I've no idea what to give Gran, though.'

'How about a mobile phone?' said Tom bitterly.

'Oh, she bought herself a smartphone last month. She's well up to date, is Gran.'

Illumination burst upon Tom like a summer dawn. 'Does she know how to text?'

'First thing she learnt. She never stops!
She's always texting her buddies at the
luncheon club.'

'Well, that's excellent! Just a minute!'
Tom dived into the fridge for the bottle of
white wine, and, grinning as widely as a
Cheshire cat, poured them each a glass.
'Here's to us, and to your Gran!'

'But why the celebration?' asked Zoe.
She couldn't help smiling back.

'I'm celebrating being married to you,'
said Tom. 'Because you're–'
He took a deep breath, and said it.
'You're wonderful, Zoe. I'm lucky to
have you.'

'Oh, Tom!' Her eyes were glistening; and
then she was in his arms, and murmuring
words he could not hear.

'What's that?' he asked tenderly, as he held her close.

'Nothing.' But Zoe repeated her thought silently, inside her head: it just shows the power of positive thinking...

She'd almost given up hope of hearing endearments from Tom. So demoralised had she become that when she found her ancient mobile, still with a pound or two of credit on it, she had started texting those silly messages to herself to boost her spirits.

The credit was used up now. But somehow, magically, it had worked. She'd been so happy when Tom started to take an interest in her again....

'Amazing,' murmured Zoe.

'Yes, you are,' said Tom.

Crime by Candlelight

Last week I walked past the old church again.
It's been turned into a nursery school now:
I could hear children's voices singing with
shrill enthusiasm. Nan would have liked that.

I strolled around the side of the building, to
see if they'd mended the window. They had,
of course. After all, it was ten years since
I'd last come down this street. I'd been living
on the other side of the country, first training
and then working as a nurse. Visits to my
childhood home were fleeting.

Over those busy years, I'd put the past behind
me. Now the sight of the church brought back
a rush of guilty memories – memories of Nan:
and Brad.

In an instant, I was sixteen again, wearing
the short skirt that made my mother wince,

and covered in more make-up than a cosmetics counter.

The skirt and the make-up were for Brad. I'd been fancying him for ages on the quiet. So when he walked up to me outside the newsagent with that swagger of his, and started chatting, I was ecstatic.

I would have done anything to keep him by my side. I would have climbed the school clock tower for him. I would have walked a tightrope across a vat of custard.

Actually, all he wanted me to do was nick a bar of chocolate while he bought cigarettes. So that was easy. Afterwards we stood under the bus shelter and shared the chocolate.

'I'm Katie,' I said.

'I know,' he said, and offered me a cigarette. I didn't smoke, but I pretended to.

Mum would have killed me: but I wasn't talking to Mum since that argument over A-level revision.

Being out with Brad was a lot more fun than sitting at home studying. Sometimes we went bowling, or to the pictures, but more often than not we just lurked around the streets having a laugh.

Brad's idea of a laugh, though, was different to mine. At first I didn't mind: no-one was going to miss the odd bar of chocolate, after all. But I wasn't so happy when he made me walk out of the supermarket with a whole bottle of wine under my coat. I didn't even drink wine! And I was sure I was going to get nabbed.

Then it started to get really serious.

'I wouldn't rob a **house**,' Brad explained.

He was jangling a pair of keys in his hand: one huge, rusty key, and one little brass one, joined by an iron ring. 'But a shop's different, and so is this place.'

'But this is a church!' I said.

'It's an empty church,' he said impatiently. 'They're building a new one down the road, and selling this place off. Nobody uses it.'

'Well, there'll be nothing worth nicking then, will there?'

'That's where you're wrong!' Brad jangled the keys again, in front of my face. 'Danny's brother works for the estate agent. He's lent me these for a couple of days. There's some interesting stuff in there, he says. No-one's got round to moving it yet, and as long as he can't be fingered for it he'll split the takings.'

'But my grandmother used to go to that church,' I protested.

My Nan had died the previous year, but the church had been her second home. Every Sunday she would trot down there, a tiny, upright figure swamped in her best blue wool coat, her felt hat squarely on her head. I remembered how she'd urge me to go too.

'Fancy coming with me this Sunday, Katie?' she'd say, with a twinkle in her eye because she knew what the answer would be.
'Ah, well. I'll say a prayer for you, my little wild child.' She was a character, my Nan. She had a sharp tongue, but she'd always help me out when I got into trouble. I missed her.

'Are you worried you're going to bump into your Nan's ghost or something?' jeered Brad.

'I'm just not comfortable about robbing a church,' I said.

'Don't be so soft! Come on. Let's take a look inside.'

The key scraped in the lock and the heavy door swung open with a creak. The place was full of musty gloom and shadows. Brad flicked a switch: but there was no electricity. A dim twilight leaked through the stained glass windows and fell on the rows of silent pews.

'There's nothing here,' I said. Apart from the empty, dusty pews, there was only a heavy lectern on a platform, along with a bare table.

Brad ignored me. He was already heading up the silent aisle, and I followed him reluctantly. A sudden rattle made me jump; but it was just a window, swinging in the breeze.

Brad scrambled onto the platform and began to rock the lectern to and fro. It had some lovely carving down the front, wooden leaves and flowers all twined together.

'That's solid oak, I reckon!' he declared. 'It'll be worth a bit. An antiques dealer might be interested.'

'We can't steal that!' I said in horror. 'I mean – it's way too heavy!'

'Danny's got a van. His brother said there's a load of candlesticks locked in a cupboard. Now I wonder where – aha! There it is!' There was a cupboard under the rattling window. Brad used the little brass key to open it.

'This is more like it! These are silver!' As he pulled out the tall candlesticks, he grinned like a shark. I think that was the moment I began to go off him.

There were some silver dishes stored in there too, and a beautiful silver cup, wrapped in a white cloth.

A chilly draught blew through the window, making me shiver. I felt really uneasy. Whatever would my Nan have said? She'd have given Brad a piece of her mind, for sure. But I wasn't brave enough to do that. I just said feebly,

'Leave it, Brad! Let's put it back. This is wrong.'

He frowned at me. 'How come you're so squeamish all of a sudden? You were happy enough to nick those cigarettes!'

I couldn't answer that. This felt far worse than stealing sweets and cigarettes: but of course, that was equally wrong. Stealing anything was wrong. I knew that. I'd just decided not to think about it – until now.

'We can't take all this lot, Brad!' I wailed. 'Somebody'll see us!'

'Stop whining,' he said impatiently. 'Of course we can't take it now. But we'll come back with Danny's van later when it's dark.'

'I'm not coming back. You can count me out!'

He glanced at me contemptuously. 'Lost your nerve, have you? Suit yourself, Miss Prim and Prissy! There's plenty of other fish in the sea.' Shovelling the silverware carelessly back into the cupboard, he pushed the door to, then stood up, rattling the keys.

'Well, off you go, then!' he sneered. 'Run home to your mummy like a good little girl. I don't need you for this job. Give me a ring when you've decided to grow up a bit.' He eyed me up and down, and then added, 'On second thoughts, don't. You're not grown up enough for me anyway.'

I knew what he meant. I'd never let him do all the things he wanted. I almost begged him for another chance; but his look of scorn made me think twice. I got out of there.

I slunk home like a kicked dog. Plodding up to my bedroom, I got my school books out, to my mum's surprise; although I couldn't concentrate on them.

All I could think of was my Nan. I imagined her face if she'd seen me in that church – and if she'd heard Brad talking about robbing it.

And then I began to imagine that she'd seen me in those shops, putting sweets in my pocket, and that bottle of wine under my coat, and hanging round the off-licence sharing stolen cigarettes with Brad. I wondered what she would think of Brad; and of me.

Straight away I knew the answer. **Not a lot.**

Those sharp, kindly eyes would have stopped twinkling at me if she'd known what I was up to.

I closed my book and stared out of the bedroom window. Moonlight filled the back garden with strange shapes, making it look haunted. Brad would be back with the van and prowling round the church before long...

I paused, thinking. Then I sprang up, flung on my black jacket, crammed my black woolly hat on my head and crept downstairs.

Mum had the telly on in the lounge. I didn't disturb her; I pulled on my boots and slipped silently out.

As I ran down the road towards the church, I knew this was a daft idea. I should really call the police and tell them about Brad. But I hated the thought of being labelled a grass.

So I had a different solution. I would get
that silverware out of the church before
Brad arrived, and hide it from his reach.

He hadn't locked the cupboard; he hadn't
even closed it properly – because he had the
key to the church, after all, and no-one else
could get in. Or so he thought... but he was
wrong.

I remembered that draughty, rattling window
over the cupboard. It hadn't been closed
properly either.

That side of the church was in shadow. No
houses overlooked it. I dragged a rainwater
butt over to the window and clambered on to
it, wobbling alarmingly.

I nearly fell off as I scrambled up to the
window, pushed it open, and with scraped
knees and skinned knuckles, managed to
haul myself inside.

I dropped down on top of the cupboard, and then began to berate myself, because it was pitch black in here and I hadn't thought to bring a torch along. I didn't even have my phone; I'd left it on my bed in my hurry. All I had in my pocket was a cheap lighter – the only present Brad had ever given me.

I could hardly see anything by its tiny flame. So I opened the cupboard and dragged out two massive candlesticks. There were several candle stubs in there as well: I carried them over to the table, set the candles in the candlesticks and lit them.

They filled the church with an eerie, flickering light. Shadows seemed to move in the pews. One shadow in particular caught my eye – it looked so strangely like a little, upright lady in a square hat and a big coat...

Picking up a candlestick, I walked down the aisle. The shadow vanished as I approached.

When I returned to the cupboard, though, and looked back, there it was again, half way down the pew, sitting watching me. In fact, I felt like the whole church was watching me.

I don't know why I wasn't more scared, alone in an empty church at midnight. But I didn't have time to be frightened: all I could think about was getting that silver out of the way before Brad arrived.

So I placed the candlesticks back on the table, and by their wavering light I emptied the cupboard of the rest of its contents. I put the bundle of silverware on top of the cupboard while I looked around for anything else that needed rescuing.

That lectern! Maybe I could move it before Brad got here. I tried to shift it, but it weighed a ton. I only managed to shuffle it to the edge of the platform before I realised that the task was beyond me.

I had just stopped to consider when I heard a sound that scared me far more than all the shadows. A key was scraping in the lock.

As the church door creaked open, I panicked. I had no time to get to the window and climb out. So I ducked down behind the lectern to hide.

Next minute, though, I realised to my horror that I'd left the candles burning – and all the silverware was still lying on top of the cupboard. But it was too late now: I was stuck behind the lectern, while heavy footsteps echoed down the aisle.

The carved foliage of the lectern had small holes amongst the leaves. Peering through one, I could just see Brad as he walked slowly down between the pews. When he stopped to stare, I kept as still as I possibly could. However, it wasn't me that Brad was staring at.

With his eyes fixed on the pair of flickering candles, he muttered, 'What the devil...?'

Then he raised his voice angrily.
'Who's there? I know you're hiding!
Where are you?'

Other than the pews down which he had just walked, there was only one place for anyone to hide. He frowned at the lectern. Crouching behind it, I began to tremble.

He was coming closer. I got ready to run, but I knew that Brad was bigger and faster than me – and that his mate Danny would be waiting outside with the van. Now I was scared: scared of Brad, because I knew what he was like...

He had reached the lectern. He grabbed it, pulling himself up on to the platform to look behind it – and then the candles both went out.

It must have been a draught from the window, for I felt a cool, strong breeze rush past me.

Surprised by the sudden darkness, Brad cried out and clutched at the lectern. It swayed and teetered as he lost his balance. He toppled backwards off the platform, and the heavy lectern followed him. I heard a thunderous crash; and then Brad groaning.

I was standing stunned, frozen to the spot, when I seemed to hear a brisk, familiar voice speaking close to my ear.
'Off you go, now, Katie!'

So I ran. I ran towards the moonlight glimmering through the window.
I scrambled up to it with a clatter of silver underfoot, squeezed through the opening and dropped down on the other side.

Then I raced off in the direction opposite to the van parked close by.

At the nearest phone box, I dialled 999 with shaking fingers and blurted out a request for an ambulance and the police.

When they asked for my name, I put the phone down and stumbled home.

I was already back in my bedroom when I heard the distant sirens wailing. Only then did it hit me, as I huddled on my bed.

That familiar voice I'd heard inside the church was just my imagination: it had to be.

But what about the breeze that had blown the candles out? That bothered me. For it had been blowing the wrong way.

It had come not from the open window, but from the shadowy rows of empty pews.
Or pews that had seemed empty...

That must be my imagination too.

None the less, as I listened to the sirens start up again and fade away, I whispered to the dark.

'Thank you, Nan, oh, thank you!'

Now, ten years later, in the sunshine with the children singing, I gazed at the old church, and whispered the same heartfelt words.

'Thank you, Nan.'

And just for an instant, in the shadows by the door, I thought I glimpsed a tiny, friendly figure swamped by her best blue coat, before I turned away.

Ellie's New Friend

'My new friend is called Daisy,' said Ellie. 'She lives in a lovely house with pink curtains with stars on them.'

'That's nice,' said Rob automatically. He didn't know any of Ellie's five year old friends, and he didn't want to hear about them right now. He had something important to tell his daughter, and only a short time to do it.

Ellie began to skip down the path. 'Daisy's got a baby bunny-rabbit and a hamster.'

'Lucky girl,' said Rob. 'Let's sit down here, shall we?'

She perched on the bench beside him and gazed dreamily across the pond.

'Daisy's got a lovely big toy boat,' she said.

'And sometimes she goes on a real boat on holiday with her Mummy and Daddy.'

Rob saw his chance. 'I might be going on holiday soon, Ellie. Actually, more than a holiday. I might go to live in Sydney.'

She stared at him. 'Is Sydney a long way away?'

'Only a few hours' drive.'

'Why are you going there, Daddy?'

'Daddy wants to earn more money,' said Rob. He wasn't doing too badly in his present job; but he was ambitious.

His wife Cara had never understood. It had been one of the reasons why they'd separated. She didn't realise that some chances never came again.

His daughter was silent for a while.

'Daisy's daddy has a job at the shops,' she said. 'Sometimes he picks Daisy up from school and takes her to his shop and she plays at shop-keeping. It's lots of fun.'

'Do you play with that new toy shop I gave you?' Rob asked. 'With the till and the scales?'

'It's nice,' said Ellie. 'Can you play shops with me today at home, Daddy?'

Rob's heart sank at the idea of counting cents and weighing plastic apples. And if he lingered at Cara's place, Cara would start going on about his move to Sydney.

She'd already been asking how Ellie would get to see him every weekend. Rob had explained that Sydney was where the opportunities were.

But Cara had just said, 'How about Ellie's opportunity to have a father?'

'Daisy's daddy gave her some real scales,' said Ellie. 'He showed her how to weigh things. They do lots of cooking together.'

'We have some beaut meals together, don't we, Ellie? Do you remember that smart restaurant I took you to last month?'

'Yes,' said Ellie flatly, before her face lit up again. 'Daisy's daddy took her to the park.'

'We're having a nice time in the park now, aren't we, honey?'

'It was a special park,' said Ellie. 'They spent all day there. They fed baby animals together.'

'Maybe we'll go there too some time,' Rob promised.

'Can we spend all day there?'

'Mmm. Time to take you back to your Mum now, sweetheart.'

'Will you stay for tea?'

'Not today. Daddy's very busy, earning lots of money. I don't suppose Daisy's daddy makes much money, does he, in a shop? I bet he can't buy Daisy a great big doll's house like the one you got for Christmas.'

'He made one with Daisy,' she said. 'Out of a shoe box. They painted it together.'

'A shoe box!' Rob laughed. But Ellie was quiet as they walked back home.

Back at the house, Cara asked him, 'Will you stay for tea? Ellie would love it if you could.'

'Just a cup of tea,' said Rob.

After Ellie had rushed off to find a picture she'd drawn, he said, 'I thought of buying Ellie a phone.'

'A phone? At her age? Oh, Rob! She doesn't want a phone. All she wants is you.'

'Well, I know that's not true,' grunted Rob. 'She's done nothing but go on about her friend Daisy. Daisy does this, Daisy does that. Daisy has a toy boat, apparently. Why don't I buy Ellie a radio-controlled boat? That'd show Daisy.'

Cara stared him. 'Don't you know who Daisy is?'

'No. Who?'

She picked up a doll. 'This is Daisy. You bought her last month.'

Only then did Rob remember snatching the doll up at a service station as a last-minute present.

'Ellie's living the life she wants through Daisy,' said Cara softly. 'Haven't you noticed that Daisy does everything with her daddy?'

Just then Ellie came bursting through the door. 'I found my picture of Daisy!'

Normally Rob would have said 'That's nice,' and barely glanced at it. But today he gazed at the sheet, taking in every detail.

A mother and father stood on either side of Daisy, holding her hands, in front of a house with pink, starred curtains. Daisy was smiling.

'It's Daisy's birthday,' said Ellie wistfully.

Suddenly Rob remembered that he hadn't made it home till late on Ellie's birthday.

Not just her birthday – so many other days…

Some chances never came again. He swallowed.

'I'll stay for tea today,' he told his daughter. 'I need to have a long talk with your Mum. And then we'll draw more pictures after tea – together.'

A Bracelet Made of Shells

Maira woke in the night to the sound of the storm.

Rain was hammering on the roof above her. She prayed that the blustering wind wouldn't tear off any slates: they couldn't afford more repairs.

And the nearby sea sounded high. The little row of beachside buildings would occasionally get showered by spray in a storm – but tonight the roar of the sea was so high and fierce that the thunderous waves might almost be crashing at the door...

Jumping up in panic, Maira flung on her dressing gown and ran down the narrow stairs to the shop.

'Oh, no!' Her fears were justified.

The waves were not just pushing at the door, but seeping under it in a dark, inexorable tide. Water lapped at the baskets and beach-mats piled on the shop floor.

Racing upstairs, Maira shook her sister Lynn awake, then ran back down to move everything possible out of harm's way.

She carried crates and baskets full of goods upstairs, and jammed towels and mats against the doorway to try to keep the water out.

Yet still the cold, relentless sea crept in.

* * *

'We might as well pack up now,' Lynn said despairingly.

Maira put an arm around her older sister's shoulders. Neither of them had slept that night; they had worked unceasingly to rescue stock until the tide receded.

Now the water had gone, leaving the shop floor covered in wet sand and littered with straw hats, and jewellery from displays that had toppled over.

'It's not that bad,' said Maira, trying to sound encouraging. 'At least it's clean.' It was surprisingly so; the sea had left no mud or rotten seaweed, just pale drifts of sand and tiny shells across the floor.

'We're the only place on the sea-front that got flooded,' Lynn said gloomily. 'Even Dave's café was okay, and that's lower down than us! How does **that** work?'

'The sea's a funny thing.'

'There's nothing funny about it,' wailed Lynn. Any more of this, and we'll have to close. Oh, Maira, I don't want to move away! Our roots are here – everything we know, everything we have!'

'Who said anything about moving?' said Maira bracingly. 'It'll dry out soon enough. Come on, Lynn. No point just sitting here. You brush up the sand, and I'll clean that jewellery. A bit of water won't have hurt it.'

But for all her breezy tone, Maira was deeply worried. The shop was already struggling.

Yet, like Lynn, she couldn't imagine living anywhere else; the little town had been home to generations of their family.

She glanced towards the old photo of their great-grandparents which usually hung over the till.

The photo wasn't on its hook. When Maira went to look for it, she found it lying on the floor behind the counter, its glass smashed. Quickly she moved it out of sight before it could cause Lynn more upset.

The shop had been Lynn's new start after her divorce, a few years back. Although Maira enjoyed working with Lynn, she found the job itself frustrating. She was an outdoors person. Despite her love of the sea, she had to resign herself to being stuck indoors all day selling gifts and souvenirs. What remained of them...

'All the postcards are damp!' wailed Lynn. 'And those hats are ruined!'

'The hats might dry out okay,' said Maira. 'And the bracelets are fine.' The sea could not damage those, for they were made of shells and chips of polished stone. They weren't valuable – but every little helped.

Maira piled the damp jewellery in a bowl, ready for rinsing and drying out before it went back on the stand. She pushed away the sneaking fear that it might all be a wasted effort.

Just when she thought she had gathered up all the bracelets, she noticed one lying in a sandy corner. She picked it up. It was formed from shells bound with twisted silver wire; and was exquisite.

Slipping it on her wrist, Maira studied it. Surely that hadn't been in the last delivery? She would have remembered.

'Have you seen this one before?' she asked her sister.

Lynn shook her head. 'Pretty,' she said dully.

Maira put the bracelet to her ear, as if from those tiny shells she might hear the soft voices of the sea. What a silly idea, she thought, and laughed.

Lynn looked up, her mouth trembling.
'I'm glad you can laugh about it! I haven't felt so bad since – since Granny Dora died.'

At the mention of their grandmother, Maira sobered. 'Sorry, Lynn. I don't know what got into me for a moment. We'll get through this, I promise! Let me take those things outside to dry.'

Carrying hats and beach-mats out of the shop, she laid them in the sunshine. The sky was pale and placid now after the storm. Only a few rumpled clouds remained.

Maira drew deep breaths of salty air, drinking it into her lungs, and then scrambled over the low sea-wall that had failed to hold back the tide. Slipping off her shoes, she walked barefoot across cool sand until she reached the water.

There she stood and gazed out at the restless sea, so changeable, so unknowable. Its moods and tides surged through their family's history.

Turning the bracelet on her wrist, she gazed out at a dark speck bobbing on the distant swell. Perhaps it was a seal...

Long before Maira was born, a storm at sea had taken Granny Dora's sister. Pearl's body had never been found. Poor Granny Dora, she mused, losing first her beloved sister, and then her daughter – for Maira's mother had walked out ten years ago, and never came back. Where she had gone, nobody knew.

Maira and Lynn had already been adults when it happened. None the less, it was a blow to Lynn especially. No wonder her sister felt so insecure, thought Maira; no wonder she feared the sea would sweep their livelihood away.

Yet right now the sea glittered like a velvet carpet spread enticingly with sparkling jewels. Waves nibbled Maira's toes and whispered to her:

Come on in. Take a swim.

As she gazed out to the horizon where sea melted into sky, longing swept over her. If only she could wade out into that cool, green world and lose herself... No, find herself...

She gave herself a shake. Take a swim? Right now – in that vast, icy ocean? This was no time to be dreaming! She had a hundred and one things to do.

Hurrying back to the shop, she collided with Dave from the café.

'Hello, Maira. I was just coming round to see if I could lend a hand,' he said awkwardly.

Maira smiled. 'That's kind of you.' She had lately become aware that Dave was very fond of Lynn – who, however, was too caught up in her own worries to even notice his attentions.

Nor did Lynn notice now. Instead, she set Dave to work fixing the jammed and swollen door.

'Are you all right, Lynn?' he asked her, his genial face full of concern.

'No, not really.' She didn't even look at him. 'I feel like a monster's just charged through our shop and ruined everything. We'll have to sell up if things don't improve.'

'It was only a freak tide,' protested Maira. 'And it didn't ruin everything.'

'It did its best. The sea's against us,' Lynn declared. 'We're at its mercy!'

Dave cleared his throat. 'Lynn, if you do decide to sell up,' he said, 'how about going into partnership with me? I've often thought that a gift shop in the café could work really well. There's plenty of space.'

Lynn stared at him. 'And what about all the hard work I've put in here?'

'It was just a suggestion...' He floundered under her angry glare.

Maira thought it was a good suggestion, if badly timed. For her own part, she'd give up working here like a shot if it wasn't for Lynn.

She had recently heard about an opening at the seal sanctuary round the bay, out in the fresh air; just the job for her. The sanctuary's owner had practically offered her the post, knowing that she found seals fascinating.

But Maira hadn't mentioned the job to Lynn yet. And if she brought it up now, it would seem like a betrayal.

So Maira resigned herself to silence. All that day she cleaned the shop, before falling into bed exhausted.

Sea-mist curled through the open bedroom window, laying a thin grey veil across her room. Yawning, she realised that the delicate shell bracelet was still on her wrist. Well, it didn't matter for one night.

As she drifted into sleep, faint faraway voices seemed to murmur lullabys to her. She dreamt that she lay softly in the cradle of the deep, being rocked as gently as a baby.

Maira woke early, still feeling the soothing sway of waves, and was momentarily bewildered to see the ceiling above her head instead of sky. Then, remembering she had a task to do before Lynn woke, she dressed quickly and hurried downstairs.

She needed a new frame for the family photo. There were plenty of frames amongst their stock, safe on a high shelf; although, strangely, they were now damp. Maira was sure they had been dry yesterday.

Maybe it was the sea-mist... She realised that the shop smelt of seaweed, and that a new, fine layer of sand lay on the floor. Where on earth had **that** come from? Maira sighed, and examined the photo.

Great-grandfather George, standing by the sepia quayside in his heavy sailor's jersey, had a look of Lynn. He held the hand of a small girl, whose face was blurred. That must be Granny Dora's sister Pearl; the one who'd drowned.

Their great-grandmother, despite her long black skirt, looked rather like Maira. Her dark hair had been made wild by the wind: strands flew out against the backdrop of the waves. She was holding a baby – Granny Dora – but her face was half turned away, towards the sea.

Carefully Maira removed the photo from its broken frame and shattered glass.

It had been in that frame for as long as she could remember. Now, on the back of the photograph, she saw for the first time two sets of words.

The first, in an unsteady hand, must have been written by Great-Grandfather George, for it said:

me and my silvie 1924 before she went home

Underneath, she recognised Granny Dora's neater writing:

George 1888-1949
Jennie, found in 1917, gone 1925
Pearl gone 1946

'What?' said Maira. She frowned at the inscriptions. They didn't make sense.
She knew Granny Dora's mother had been called Jennie, and had died young...

But what did it mean, **found in 1917**? And who was this Silvie? She had never heard of a Silvie in the family.

Possibilities raced through her mind. Had George had two wives, or one wife with two names? She shook her head, baffled. Well, it was all a long time ago. It hardly mattered now.

But the photo meant a lot to Lynn. So, fitting it carefully into its new frame, Maira hung it in its old place on the wall.

Then she swept up the latest drift of sand, while a soft voice whispered in her head:

My Silvie. My Silvie.

By the time Lynn came downstairs, the sand was gone; but Lynn was horrified to find everything so damp.

'Look at those calendars, all curled up!' she wailed. 'They were fine yesterday! Whatever happened? We can't sell those!'

Maira didn't like to point out that, in truth, there was hardly anyone around to buy them. They saw only a dozen customers all day. The recent bad weather had put tourists off.

One of the few that came in commented to Maira, 'I love that pretty bracelet that you're wearing. Have you got another one the same?'

Maira knew she ought to take off the shell bracelet and offer it to her customer. But she felt a strange reluctance to give it up.

'We have some very similar,' she said, showing her the jewellery stand. But in the end, the woman – like nearly all the other customers – walked out empty-handed.

Next day brought yet more sand and even fewer visitors. Once more Maira swept up secretly, before Lynn came downstairs. She fingered the curling postcards in bewilderment.

Sea-mist... But how had all this sand blown in? The wind had dropped, yet sand had still seeped past the doors. It was as if the sea really was against them...

All day, sorting through the stock, Maira's head felt clouded. As she turned the bracelet on her wrist, she heard the gulls' plaintive calls, summoning her outside.

She could not concentrate, and was relieved when Lynn announced that they might as well close early.

'I'm going for a coffee at Dave's,' said Lynn. 'Are you coming. Maira?'

'No, I'll join you later,' she told her sister. 'First I'll have a walk and clear my head.'

Maira took the coast path and headed for the cliffs.   The walk wasn't merely to clear her head. There was something up there that she wanted to check.

So she trudged up the sloping track to the little grey church that huddled on the cliff-top, its graveyard gathered around it like a skirt, while the sea swept the beach far below.

It was a wild and lonely spot for a graveyard, but Maira loved it for its wide views of the endless sea. Seagulls wailed as she slowly strolled amongst the graves.

It took her a while to find the gravestone. She hadn't looked for it for some time, and it was overgrown and almost hidden. Parting the long grass, she read the inscription.

Here lay George, as she had remembered –
but not his wife. She searched nearby,
without finding any headstone for Jennie.
No mention of a Silvie was to be found here
either. George's wife – or maybe wives –
remained a mystery.

Walking over to the cliff edge, Maira gazed
out across the wide, bright, shifting sea.
It looked so alluring that she had to remind
herself how perilous it was. It had taken
Granny Dora's sister...

A dark shape bobbed in the waves beneath
her: the head of a distant seal. She turned
the bracelet on her arm.

'**Come and join us, come into the water...** '

The murmurs were as faint as sea-mist.
The seal watched her from far below.
As if in a dream, Maira took a pace forward,
and another.

Then, coming to her senses with a jolt, she took a sharp breath. What was she thinking of? She stepped back quickly from the cliff-edge, and hurried down the hill.

* * *

'I saw a seal out in the bay,' she told Lynn in the cafe, hoping to turn the conversation to the job at the seal sanctuary.

But Lynn sniffed. 'You and your seals! I've decided we'll do a full stock-take, starting tomorrow. We'll go through everything and see what stock we need to re-order – if we can afford it.'

Dave, bringing Maira's coffee over to the table, said, 'No, you have a day off, Lynn. You need it. Tell you what, I'll take you both out somewhere.'

He cast an appealing look at Maira, who said promptly, 'That'd be brilliant!

We could do with a break. A day off would recharge our batteries, wouldn't it, Lynn?' Reluctantly, Lynn agreed.

Dave beamed. 'Right, then! It's a date. I'll arrange something that you'll enjoy.'

The next day dawned calm and clear. The smooth, peaceful sea glimmered like mother-of-pearl.

'Perfect day for a boat ride,' said Dave when they met up. 'I thought we'd go out on the Seal Boat – you know, the one that takes tourists round the bay. And then we'll go for fish and chips. How does that sound?'

Lynn looked unconvinced. She wasn't as keen on seals as Maira.

But they coaxed her into the boat, where they sat amidst eager seal-spotters as it chugged across the flat calm of the bay.

'You can barely see our shop from here,' said Maira. She wished she hadn't mentioned it when Lynn grunted,

'It won't be our shop for much longer, if the sea has its way.'

'Look,' said Dave, pointing in the opposite direction, 'there are the seals!'

Half a dozen sleek heads poked out of the water. There was a general cry of delight. The seals were watching them with liquid brown eyes; and Maira was as entranced as the other occupants of the boat.

But beside her, Lynn gasped suddenly in alarm. 'What's **that**?'

She pointed, and Maira stared across the glittering water. At first she thought, incredulously, that an enormous silver serpent lay stretched out across the sea.

She had only a second in which to think, 'Why, it's a wave–' before it was upon them.

It rushed on them at speed, reared up and swamped the boat. Along with everyone else, Maira was flung into the water.

After the shock of cold, she felt no alarm. She was a good swimmer; but she let herself drift underwater, held in the strong arms of the sea. Here was another world, timeless, dim and tranquil.

Somebody was there with her. Brown eyes met hers; a sleek brown body swam past.

A seal. She put out a hand and touched it. Its nose nudged her. **Up! Up!**

Then she remembered Lynn. In a sudden panic she kicked her way upwards until her head emerged into air and noise and daylight.

People were screaming. Lifebelts were being thrown, splashing into the waves.

'Lynn?' cried Maira. 'Lynn! Where are you?' She dived to look for her sister. But the seal was still down there in the dim water, and pushed her up again.

This time, as her head broke the surface, she saw Lynn. Dave was holding her up. Somehow he'd got a life-jacket on her. Lynn's face was white but her eyes were open: Dave propelled her to the life-raft that was rapidly inflating nearby.

She's safe, thought Maira. Now I can go.

And she let herself slide back underwater, into the cool green depths she so desired. This was where she wanted to be.

But once again a firm brown body pushed against her. The seal had other ideas.

Its snout was at her wrist, its sharp teeth pulling at the bracelet.

Then she found herself at the surface again, gasping and spluttering, and barely aware of the strong hands that grabbed at her clothes and hauled her out, until she lay shivering in the life-raft.

Lynn hugged her. 'Oh, thank goodness you're all right, Maira! I thought you'd drowned. Dave saved us both.' And Lynn turned to the bedraggled Dave, leaned her head upon his shoulder and began to weep. Dave gently stroked her dripping hair.

Maira touched the bracelet on her wrist. The seal hadn't bitten through it, though it had loosened it. She pulled it off and slumped back, feeling dazed.

What had she been thinking of, there in the water?

Had she really been so ready to slip down into the cool depths of the sea? As if she could ever do that to Lynn…

She gazed out at the water, which was now as smooth as silk – as tranquil as if the freak wave had never been. A head broke the surface: a pair of dark eyes gazed back at her, before they disappeared without a ripple.

Maira clutched the bracelet and let the sea surge through her head. Those eyes.
My Silvie…

* * *

'I think working at the Seal Sanctuary's a great idea,' said Lynn. 'I was so worried about leaving you with nothing if I closed the shop. I felt I couldn't do that to you.'

It was three weeks later, and they were emptying the shop for good – with Dave's assistance.

Where once Lynn would have ignored him, now she never stopped asking his advice. It was as if the giant wave had washed them together: they were inseparable.

'You won't need my help once you and Dave join forces at the cafe,' said Maira, smiling.

'But if Dave and I move in together...' Lynn was blushing.

'Don't worry, you can let the lease go. There's a small flat I can rent near the sanctuary that would suit me fine.'

'Oh, good! But Maira, do take anything you like from here.'

Maira looked around the shop. Truth to tell, she wasn't particularly attached to any of the belongings. There was only one thing that she really wanted.

'Could I have that family photo, do you think?' she asked. 'I'll make you a copy.'

'If that's what you want – sure.' Lifting the picture from the wall, Lynn handed it over.

Maira gazed down at George and his wife. Looking closely at the photograph, for the first time she noticed something on the woman's wrist. Was it a bracelet?
It was hard to tell.

But Maira recognised the longing in the woman's face as she half-turned her head, looking out to sea. Granny Dora had known her mother's secret. Now Maira knew it too.

Jennie was gazing out across the waves that she had come from, and to which she would soon return. Years later, her daughter Pearl would follow her. More than likely that was where her grand-child, Maira's mother, had gone too...

One day Maira might find out. One day, when she put the bracelet back upon her wrist. But she would not do that yet. Not for many years.

George must have found his wife when he was in his fishing-boat, amongst the seals out in the bay.

Perhaps he had discovered her entangled in his net; perhaps she had swum up to the boat to watch him with brown, liquid eyes, and they had caught each other...

She had travelled back to shore with him, had given herself a human name and married him; but she had always heard the sea calling.

In the end, its call had been too strong for her – as it had been for one in every generation since.

Dave and Lynn will have daughters, Maira thought. One will be special: she'll love the sea. She'll be a child of the seal-people out of ancient tales, just like her great-great-grandmother Jennie in the photograph.

Just like Pearl, who answered the sea's call. Just like my mother.

Just like me.

Outside, Maira heard the waves' long, wistful sigh. She carefully took the photo from the frame and turned it over.

Even before she re-read the inscription, she knew what she would see. She'd been mistaken when she read the words before. The answer had been there all along.

For George's shaky writing did not say **my silvie**, but **my silkie**.

Life in the Fast Lane

'Hey! Stop, thief!'

At the shout, Kenny panicked. He'd been clumsy. His victim had felt the purse slide from her bag.

He could easily outrun the old woman, though. The passers-by would never catch him. The only people round here at this hour were other old ladies – apart from one man who'd just gone into a shop...

And who had left his car parked only yards away. He'd even left the keys in! Another white-haired woman – probably his mum – sat in the passenger seat.

That's a good fast car for a getaway, thought Kenny. Next second he had flung the car door open.

He threw himself into the driver's seat and drove off with a screech of tyres. Its owner ran out of the shop, too late. With a rude gesture, Kenny sped triumphantly away.

Beside him, the old lady clutched her handbag. Kenny decided that once he was safely away from the scene of his crime, he'd stop the car and pitch her out.

'Aren't you doing up your seat belt?'

'My seat belt?' Kenny frowned at her. The daft old bird couldn't have understood what was happening. 'This is a car-jacking!' he growled, and turned to look for pursuers.

'**Mirrors**,' the old lady said.

'What?'

'Please use your mirrors.'

Crazy, he thought. He rounded a corner wildly. The car mounted the pavement before jolting to a stop.

'Out you get!' he snapped.

'Dear me,' said the old lady, fumbling with her door, 'I can't. I think you must have put the child lock on.'

Kenny swore. He could hear a distant police siren. It might be nothing to do with him – but he didn't want to stick around to find out.

'Forget it!' He put his foot down. The car bounded forward like a drunken kangaroo.

'Steady on the clutch,' said the old lady calmly. 'I'm Patty.'

Batty, more like, thought Kenny as he clashed the gears.

'Where are you going?' she asked.

'Shut up! I'm not a taxi service!'

But which way should he go? Anywhere away from that siren...

Kenny swerved erratically, nearly hit a van, and bumped over the middle of a roundabout. They hurtled down a quiet street, narrowly missing several parked cars.

'The speed limit's thirty miles an hour here,' said Patty.

'Not for me,' snorted Kenny. She'd probably never travelled at more than thirty in her life. Well, she was about to discover life in the fast lane! He'd show her what a real driver could do. He grinned.

'Hold tight!' Crashing the gears, he put his foot down. The engine shrieked in complaint.

Patty reached into her handbag.

'Stop that!' said Kenny sharply. She must be looking for her phone. She wasn't ringing anyone! He grabbed the bag and flung it in the foot-well.

That police siren was getting closer. Cursing, Kenny shot through a red light and onto the main road. Several cars braked, their drivers looking startled. Patty waved at them apologetically.

'For crying out loud!' rasped Kenny.

'Good manners never hurt.'

'Well, thanks for the tip,' he jeered, cutting in front of a van.

To his dismay, he suddenly saw blue flashing lights not far ahead. Time for a U-turn! Kenny spun the wheel.

The car skidded sickeningly, out of control. He wrenched the wheel this way and that, but it wouldn't obey.

He was skidding right across the road at high speed, with a heavy truck bearing down on him. Its horn blasted like an elephant's trumpet....

Patty seized the steering wheel. Kenny screamed. She was trying to kill him! All around them, brakes were squealing. He closed his eyes tight, waiting for the crunch...

With no seatbelt to hold him, he was thrown heavily sideways.

Then the car stopped. He opened his eyes.

The huge truck was a hair's breadth from his bonnet – and right behind him was a police car. He was trapped.

Patty reached past him to switch off the engine.

'Thank you for the drive,' she said. 'Much more exciting than the one I was expecting. Just let me give you something...'

While she rummaged in her handbag, Kenny groaned. He couldn't move. He was sure he'd broken all his ribs.

'Here you are,' said Patty. 'And remember: always steer into a skid.'

She hopped out. Kenny stared down at her card. It read:

'Patty Penn – Advanced Driving Lessons.'

Mushrooms

Nettie turned the mushroom over, carefully
inspecting the gills before putting it in her
basket. It wouldn't do to feed the wrong
ones to her husband Ged.

But she'd been picking them for years.
She knew exactly what to look for.
And she enjoyed this peaceful task,
in the soothing tranquillity of the woods
at the edge of town.

'How do you tell which ones are safe to eat
and which ones aren't?'

Nettie glanced up in surprise. It wasn't
often that she encountered anyone else here.
Mushroom pickers were few and far between.

And this man didn't look the part, in his
smart black overcoat.

He was dressed more for a business meeting than for getting down on his knees on damp grass. Smiling widely at her, he said politely,

'I'm a novice at this. Can you give me any pointers?'

'Well, these brown ones with thick stems are called ceps,' said Nettie. 'These are perfectly good to eat. But make sure you don't pick any of **those**.'

She pointed to a clump of greenish-brown ones. 'Those are death caps. They're fairly common around here – but definitely to be avoided! Just one of those can kill an adult.'

'They look like ordinary field mushrooms,' he commented.

She shook her head, and turned one of the death caps over to show him.

'Look for the white gills. It's all too easy to make a mistake. If in doubt, leave it out.'

'Thanks.' The man produced a plastic bag and began to pick.

Nettie resumed her own harvesting, glancing over at him from time to time.

'Not that one!' she said warningly. 'Look at the white gills! That's a death cap.'

'Whoops! My mistake.' He threw the mushroom away.

'Mushroom-picking really isn't a good idea for novices,' said Nettie; but the man seemed not to hear. He moved further away and kept on gathering.

Once her own basket was full, she stood up to leave. The man was busy picking some distance away.

Nettie wondered if she should offer to check his crop. He had left his bag by the path, so she glanced inside it.

It was full of death caps. The white gills were plain to see. Weren't they obvious to him? How could he make such a mistake?

She opened her mouth to warn him. He was rummaging fiercely in a drift of dead leaves. As she watched, he pounced on another find and held it up with triumph. Even from a distance, Nettie could see it was a death cap.

She swallowed and backed away, walking hurriedly down the path. At the edge of the wood, she paused behind a thick clump of bushes.

Ten minutes later, the man walked past, swinging his bag and whistling. Nettie began to follow some way behind.

It was possible he'd picked them for an innocuous reason; but she needed to be sure. So she trailed him into town.

Once they reached the main road, the rush-hour crowds camouflaged her and she was able to get close behind him. But she was nearly caught out when he stopped abruptly in a doorway.

Nettie swiftly turned to study a shop window, her heart thumping, praying he wouldn't recognise her.

Luckily he wasn't looking at her. He was intent on answering his mobile phone.

'Suze! Listen, babe, I'll see you later. Laura's expecting me home half an hour ago. Don't worry! I know what I promised. I said I'd sort her out, and I will, once and for all.'

The call did nothing to calm Nettie's thudding heart. Her legs felt weak as she forced herself to continue following him.

He turned down a driveway leading to a large house. Nettie crept round to the back and gazed at the brightly lit windows. Dusk was falling; she trusted that she could not be seen.

But she could see him, in the kitchen, talking to a woman – Laura? Although she couldn't hear them, she could read their conversation. He was offering to cook dinner. Laura reacted with surprise; it obviously wasn't something he did often.

Nettie waited until he was busy chopping onions before she rang the front doorbell.

Laura came to the door. She had a tired, worn face, with a blue bruise on one cheekbone.

'I've been picking mushrooms in the woods,' said Nettie.

'I don't think we –'

'Ssh! Your husband was there, picking too. If he offers you mushrooms for dinner, don't eat them.'

Laura's eyes grew wide. She took a gasping breath, and closed the door.

Had she understood? wondered Nettie. Then a light went on in an upstairs room. She looked up and saw Laura pulling down a suitcase from on top of a wardrobe, and starting to stuff clothes into it.

Nettie nodded and hurried away down the drive. Laura had understood, all right. She'd been shocked: but she hadn't been surprised. Laura had seen the signs, thought Nettie, as she reached her own house.

And Nettie, in turn, had recognised the signs in Laura's bruised, unhappy face that all was far from well within her marriage.

She emptied her bag of mushrooms into the sink to wash them. She'd recognised the signs; because she'd seen them so often in the mirror. She touched a hand to her cheek.

'Is that you?' she heard Ged shout. 'About time too. When's tea?'

'Soon,' she called back, as she began to wash the mushrooms.

She'd been careful to pick the right ones this time. Ged would never think to check the gills. He wouldn't know a death cap from a doughnut.

As for Nettie, she never ate mushrooms.

Auntie Amy's Answers

'What we need,' said Michael decisively,
'is a new look. Something eye-catching!
Attention-grabbing! Now, I've got a few
ideas.'

Lucy saw the other committee members
round the table glance at each other. She
grinned. Michael always had a few ideas.

When he'd taken over as minister in the
quiet parish of Hebstone, nobody had
expected this friendly, absent-minded
man to make any sweeping changes.

But first he'd replaced the dwindling
Sunday School with a raucous Fun Club.
Next came the Friday night discos for the
under-eighteens, and then the over-fifties
tea-dances which quickly developed their
own discos as a sideline.

Yet despite all the upheaval, he was a popular minister. You couldn't help liking him, Lucy decided. He and Simon would have been great friends.

Briefly, she dropped her head at the thought of her late husband. Simon had only been in his forties: far too young... After six years alone, her grief had turned to quiet reflection. Nevertheless, sometimes she was lonely.

Lucy ticked herself off. She had a great job at the Citizens' Advice Bureau. And the parish committee was a good antidote for loneliness. She had to admit that Michael was making the meetings a lot more interesting.

So far, she hadn't been involved in his changes. Her son Adam was too old for the discos, while she herself was too young for the tea dances. She looked up again, smiling in anticipation. So what was Michael's latest bright idea?

Michael slapped the latest copy of the parish magazine down on the table. 'It needs a facelift,' he said.

'I do my best with it,' said Janice apologetically. 'It's just hard finding enough news to fill it.'

'You've done a great job, Janice,' Michael reassured the elderly lady. 'I'd love you to keep doing the Church News. I'll write a regular column, as usual. But we need more reader appeal! We need to add some oomph!'

'What about a children's corner?' suggested Fiona tentatively.

'Brilliant idea! Would you have a go at that? And I thought a Teen page – how about it, Colin? You know all about what teenagers are into!'

Lucy was amused as Colin, father of three hulking teenagers, looked aghast. 'I'll see what I can do,' he said doubtfully.

Michael leant eagerly across the table. 'And Lucy, I thought of just the thing for your talents! A problem page!'

'A problem page?'

'Admit it – doesn't everybody love to read about other people's problems? And you'd be the perfect person to dispense sensible advice, Lucy, with all your experience at the Citizens' Advice Bureau.'

It was Lucy's turn to be aghast. 'Well, maybe, but...' She floundered. 'My experience is with bus passes and tax credits! I help people fill out forms – I don't mend broken hearts!'

'Nevertheless, Lucy, something tells me you're just the right person.'

Michael smiled at her, his eyes crinkling warmly. 'You'd be anonymous, of course. You could call yourself Auntie someone. Auntie Amy's Answers – how about that? Please say you'll give it a go!'

'Well – all right,' Lucy agreed, with deep misgiving. 'I suppose that I can try.'

* * *

The new style parish magazine was duly advertised. Apprehensively, Lucy waited for the problems to flood in for her problem page. But a month later, only two letters had arrived, and neither of them was quite what she had been expecting.

'This problem page isn't going to work,' she told Michael. 'So far we've had one request for the name of a tree surgeon, and one letter asking for advice about vine weevil! Are you sure you wouldn't like a gardening page instead?'

Michael's face fell. 'Oh, dear. I really thought it might provide a useful service,' he said sadly. 'I get the feeling there are so many people who would like advice and help, but are too shy to ask for it face to face.'

'Maybe,' said Lucy. 'Maybe they're too shy to write a letter as well!'

'I don't want to give up just yet.' Then Michael's face lit up. 'Lucy, how would it be if you wrote a couple of letters yourself? Just to start the ball rolling, as it were.'

'You mean make them up?'

'I don't think it would be wrong. It would just show people the sort of thing they could write in about. It might give them confidence.'

'But what on earth should I write?' cried Lucy in consternation.

Michael smiled. 'I know you don't have any problems of your own, Lucy. But I'm sure you'll think of something!'

That evening Lucy sat at her kitchen table in despair. 'I can't do this!' she said aloud. 'I haven't got a clue what to write!'

She put her chin in her hands, wishing she had someone to talk it through with. Someone like Simon, or her down-to-earth father – although he had never read a problem page in his life.

She was flummoxed. She had no problems of her own... or did she? She frowned. After a moment she took up her pen.

'Dear Auntie Amy,' she wrote, 'I am concerned about my father, who is 81 and lives on his own some miles away. Although his health is still good, he is getting frail.

I worry about how he will cope in years to come.'

She stared across the room at the calendar her father had sent her, remembering their conversation last month. Then she wrote:

'I love my father dearly, and would be very happy for him to move in with me. But he insists on staying in his own house even though it is too big for him. What can I do?'

She got up and made herself a cup of tea. The conversation had ended in an impasse. Her father was stubborn about staying put; Lucy had found herself getting impatient.

She picked up her pen again.

'Auntie Amy's Answer:

'Try and see this from your father's point of view.

'He doesn't want to leave a house where he has lived so long and which holds happy memories. He probably knows quite well that it may have to happen eventually – but until then, do all you can to help him stay there in comfort.

'Why not ask your local Citizens Advice Bureau about Meals on Wheels and subsidised home help?'

Lucy smiled wryly as she wrote this. Then her smile faded as she added the last sentence: 'Are you sure your invitation isn't partly because you yourself are lonely?'

She stared at the page. Maybe it is, she said to herself. I never thought... I never realised it till now.

She got up and paced the kitchen. She hadn't meant to write such a revealing letter. Could she put it in the magazine?

Well, why not? After all, Michael didn't know about her father. He would assume she'd made it up.

And her father didn't read problem pages... But her next conversation with him would be different.

When the magazine appeared, Michael was delighted.

'It's just what I wanted!' he said. 'Something that people can identify with. The letters for Auntie Amy will come pouring in now, you'll see!'

'Oh, no!'

He laughed. 'Don't pull that face, Lucy! I tell you what – if it doesn't take off after three issues, we'll drop the whole idea. Agreed?'

'Agreed,' said Lucy in relief.

Time passed. No problem letters arrived. Lucy didn't know whether to be thankful or not. There was nothing for it but to make up her own letter a second time...

Once more she sat in the kitchen, sighing and biting her pen. Then she reproved herself. Her son Adam had given her this pen set for Christmas, and look at it now!

She began to write.

'Dear Auntie Amy, I am concerned about my son. He is twenty- one. I was so proud of him when he was offered a place to do medicine at university. But now, half way through his degree, he has suddenly announced that he wants to leave and do physiotherapy instead!'

Lucy frowned. Adam's decision still hurt.

'He's gone ahead and arranged to switch his course without even consulting me.

I feel upset that he didn't think it worth telling me beforehand. And I think he's throwing away a great opportunity. What should I do?'

'Oh dear,' she said aloud. 'Poor Adam. I was so short with him. But throwing away a medical career...'

She took up the pen again, not yet sure what Auntie Amy was going to reply. But the words came flowing almost faster than she could get them down.

'Auntie Amy's Answer:

'You shouldn't do anything! This is his decision. Medicine is a wonderful career, but it's not for everyone. Your son is lucky to have realised this now rather than at the end of his course. Imagine how unhappy he would be stuck in a demanding job that he didn't enjoy!

'Physiotherapy is also very rewarding and worthwhile, and your son has done well to get a place. In not consulting you, he's trying to be adult and make his own decisions! The best thing you can do is ring up and congratulate him on his maturity.
It can't have been an easy choice for him.'

Lucy stared at her words. No, it couldn't have been easy for Adam – but she hadn't really considered his feelings properly until just now. She reflected for a while, and then added,

'Is it the loss of prestige that worries you? You can't live your life through your son.'

Bother Michael and his problem page! thought Lucy, staring at the words she had just written. I never expected to end up searching my own heart like this.

Carefully she replaced the pen in its box.

'You've got to live your own life your own way, Adam,' she said aloud. 'I know that. And I've got to live mine.'

Fiona and Janice might well recognise who the letter was about – but why hide it? She was proud of Adam, and ashamed of herself. So into the magazine the letter went. If Michael guessed the truth, he was too tactful to say.

'Outstanding!' he enthused. 'What an imagination! I don't know how you do it.'

'That's the last letter that I'm writing,' said Lucy firmly. 'If no one sends in a real problem, then that's it.'

'Oh, I'm sure they will,' said Michael confidently. 'We'll have a truckload of mail – the post office won't be able to cope!'

Lucy couldn't help laughing.

'I do hope you're wrong!' she said.

'Just wait and see.'

The time for the next issue rolled around.
Lucy spoke to Michael after church.

'Well? Where's the truckload of mail?'

Michael grimaced. 'It must have been
held up.'

'That's it, then! No more Auntie Amy.'

'Hang on – there is just one letter.' Michael
pulled an envelope out of his pocket.
'You did say you'd give it three goes.'

Lucy hesitated. 'Please? For me?' Michael
implored her.

Lucy smiled. He was trying so hard, and he
was such a nice man...

'All right,' she agreed. 'Hand it over!'

Back home, she opened the letter.
The hand-writing was awkward, as if
someone was trying to disguise it.
She wondered who the writer could be.

Then she put the thought firmly out of
her mind. It wasn't any of her business.

She would do her best to help with this
problem, whatever it was. But then that
was the end. No more. She began to read.

'Dear Auntie Amy,

'You are the only person I feel able to tell
about this. I am a single man of forty-six,
working in your parish. Unexpectedly I
have found myself growing extremely fond
of a lovely lady who lives nearby. She has
no idea how I feel, and I am at a loss as to
how to broach the subject with her.

'She is a very kind, practical, independent person, and has shown no sign of wanting anyone else to share her life. She is also a widow, and I am not sure how she would feel about anyone asking her out.

'I am worried about offending her or stirring up sad memories. Please advise me. I don't know what to do.'

Lucy read the letter through again, slowly, before laying it down on the table.
She had a feeling she knew who had written this letter.

She bit her lip, pondering, and then took up her pen. It was important to get the answer right. She thought some more, and wrote:

'Auntie Amy's Answer:

'You show great sensitivity to this lady's feelings.

'I think if you said to her exactly what
you have said in your letter, she might
feel confused and unsure at first,
but she would not be offended.
Whether she would agree to go out with
you is, of course, something I cannot say!

'But I can say this. Don't be afraid of
stirring up sorrow. The sorrow of losing
her husband will always be in that lady's
heart – but you may have the means to put
new joy there too. Why not give it a go?
Be brave, and talk to her face to face!
Give her the chance to think about it,
at least!'

There: that would have to do. After all,
she couldn't be perfectly sure who the
writer was – or who he was writing about...

Next day she took the letter and reply
round to Michael's house.

'Just in time for the deadline,' he said jovially, but his face was unusually anxious. 'What did you make of the letter?'

'What did you think of it?' countered Lucy.

'Me? Um – well – quite a dilemma, poor man.'

'Michael!' she cried in mock indignation. 'Are you telling me you steamed open that letter? It was sealed when you handed it to me!'

His face was a picture.

'You wrote it, didn't you?' said Lucy gently.

He took a deep breath and nodded.

'She's a very lucky lady,' said Lucy.

Michael's voice was hoarse. 'Lucy – I wrote it about you.'

Lucy felt a strange relief: and then a delight that she hadn't felt for years, slowly unfolding inside her.

'And your answer?' implored Michael.

'It's there.' She pointed to the letter in his hand. 'I think you'll be happy with it. But that's the last answer I'm writing. No more problem pages, please!'

'We'll have a gardening page instead,' promised Michael, a joyful smile spreading across his face. 'Lucy? Thank you for doing that last letter. Nobody else could have. But something just told me you were the person – right from the start!'

Rescue Me

'Marianne! I haven't seen you for – for about three years.'

Lee almost gave himself away. He nearly said, 'three years, six months, two days.' His last meeting with Marianne was burned into his memory.

They'd been high school sweethearts for a short time, until Marianne had called it off.

'We're too young to get serious,' she said, laughing. She was always laughing back then.

Lee went away to college and tried to forget her. Then, years later, he bumped into her by accident, on the arm of a burly shaven-headed man.

'This is Carl,' said Marianne proudly.

And she showed him the engagement ring.

Lee didn't like the look of Carl, with his belligerent strut and his tattoos: but he congratulated Marianne, and then tried to forget her all over again.

The trouble was, he couldn't. Although he avoided the places she might go, and sought no news of her, she was always in his thoughts.

He had a couple of girlfriends, but they didn't last. Sometimes he wondered if he would ever get over Marianne. So seeing her on the train like this, on his way to work, was a dreadful, wonderful shock.

Marianne had changed. Her sad eyes had deep shadows under them. He noticed her wedding ring, and then the bruise on her thin arm. She looked worn out.

Lee's heart turned over. It was all he could do to say casually, 'So, how's life treating you?'

'Oh... you know. Things aren't easy these days. I just got a job at a shop in town, so that's something. But life with Carl is difficult...' The racket of the train drowned out her quiet voice.

Lee asked, 'Did – did Carl give you that bruise?'

She nodded, and Lee clenched his fists in his lap.

'I love him to bits,' Marianne went on. 'But he's so strong... Don't get me wrong! I've no regrets. I can't imagine life without him. It's just hard sometimes.'

Lee swallowed, wishing Carl was there so that he could give him a piece of his mind.

'But that's enough about me!' said Marianne. 'Tell me about you.'

He embellished it a bit. He made his job sound more high-flying than it really was.

'You've done well,' she said wistfully. 'I wish I'd gone to college. But there's no way, now.'

As they pulled into her station, she got up. 'It's been lovely seeing you again, Lee. It's good to know you're happy.'

He watched in anguish as she walked away. Happy? How could he be happy when she wasn't? He wished he could do something, anything, to help her.

What he really wanted to do was murder Carl. But that would hardly help. Carl was clearly the love of Marianne's life.

After that, Lee was careful to catch the same train every day. On Thursdays and Fridays, she caught it too. He would smile and wave, and sit next to her when he could.

Was it his imagination, or did her face lighten on seeing him? He carefully skirted round the subject of Carl, instead chatting about their school days.

'I've lost touch with most of the old crowd,' sighed Marianne. 'I don't get out much, what with working weekends… and Carl doesn't like me going out.'

'What are your neighbours like?'

'Oh, they're nice enough. The area's run down, though – and our house!' She pulled a wry face. 'It needs so much work, and the garden's a tip. I keep promising myself to get stuck in – but there's no time, or money either.'

What about Carl, the lazy so and so? thought Lee indignantly. But when he said, 'Get Carl to help you,' Marianne just laughed.

'Can you imagine the mess he'd make?' She shook her head. 'It's down to me. Maybe I'll start on it next week, while Carl's away.'

'Where's he going?'

'Oh, he's off visiting his dad. Two of a kind, they are. Big, loud bruisers.'

At the affection in her voice, Lee had to turn away.

He made an instant resolution. He would do up the garden for her.

During their chats, he'd learnt her address: while Carl was away and Marianne was working, he could secretly set to work.

So the following Saturday, Lee drove across town to her house. It was a faded end of terrace with a collapsing fence and a garden full of rubbish that had been blown in.

He cleared the plastic bags and crisp packets away, and dug out the weeds. After mowing the scrap of muddy grass he fixed the fence. The gate was broken too, but it was getting late. Marianne might be home soon: maybe he'd come back another day…

Next time he met her on the train, Marianne was glowing, eager to tell him the unexpected news about her garden.

'I can't think what happened!' she exclaimed. 'Somebody must have booked a gardener and he came to the wrong address. That's the only explanation!'

Lee agreed, and then kept quiet.

He couldn't tell her what he'd done, because he wouldn't be able to stop himself from spilling out his feelings for her. And that wouldn't be fair.

But he could mend that gate, and plant some bulbs in her bare flowerbeds. It wasn't much; but he'd do anything to make her happier.

A couple of weeks later Marianne mentioned that Carl would be away again. Once more, Lee drove over to the house and set to work.

He was busy planting bulbs when he heard a cry. Marianne's voice shouted, 'Stop, Carl! No!'

Lee froze. Carl had discovered him! He whirled round to defend himself.

Charging through the gate with a roar came a furious, bullet-headed two-year-old.

'Come back, Carl!' Marianne, running after him, stopped dead. 'Lee!' she gasped. 'You're the gardener?'

'Yes. Is **that** Carl?'

'Carl junior. I had to fetch him early – his dad reckoned he was sickening for something, but I think he was just too lazy to have him for the whole weekend like the custody agreement says. I think he's well enough, don't you?'

Lee studied little Carl, who had grabbed the trowel and was trying to dig. He was a sturdy little bruiser, all right.

And looking up at Marianne's glad, shining face, he realised that although her son might have first place in her heart, perhaps there was still room there for another.

The School Dinner Saboteur

'Oh, yuck! What's the green stuff? I'm not eating **that**.' The boy held his plate out at arm's length.

'That's broccoli,' I said sternly, giving him my hardest dinner lady's glare.

'Sorry, miss,' he stammered. 'I'm just not very hungry, that's all.'

Surveying the children in the school dining room, I thought bleakly that none of them looked very hungry. The usual happy chatter was missing: plates were pushed aside and long faces pulled.

I couldn't blame them. The broccoli had turned to mush. The meat pie looked grey and soggy. The apple sponge had fallen to bits.

With a sigh I turned back into the kitchen. My first week as the new school cook wasn't going well.

'I don't know what's going wrong,' I told Lorna, my assistant. 'It must be the ovens. Did the last cook have this trouble?'

'No – but I'm sure you'll soon get the hang of them, Cherry,' she said sympathetically.

'I'll have to,' I muttered, frowning at the gleaming steel ovens and hobs. They were only a few years old, and they should work fine. So how had they turned my carefully prepared school dinner into such an unappetising mess?

I felt bad for the children, who were gloomily pushing food around their plates before hurrying out to play.

My son, Will, was amongst them.

As he ran out, he gave me a wave – but
he looked worried.

Poor Will! I thought I'd landed the perfect
job in his new junior school. But on the
very first day his classmates had christened
me Mrs Mushy Peas. Goodness knows what
they'd be calling me now...

After clearing up and loading the vast
dishwasher, I stayed alone in the kitchen
checking the equipment. It all seemed
to work properly – now. Just not when I
had needed it to.

'Maybe it's the thermostats,' I muttered,
and began to hunt around for manuals.
I didn't find any. All I found, hidden on
a high shelf, was an old exercise book.

The cover read **Mrs Pike. MEALS**. Inside,
in crabbed handwriting, was a list of dates
and menus. The dates were in the 1980s.

The menus were grim. Liver figured largely, as did mackerel and Brussels sprouts and other things I'd definitely think twice about serving up to eight-year-olds.

As I read, there was a rustle in the corner near the fridges.

'Hey!' I put the book down and marched over, expecting to find that a child had sneaked in unseen.

But there was nobody there – just a sour smell, like old liver and cabbage. Where had **that** come from? Maybe the odours of ancient meals had worked themselves into the walls...

Shaking my head, I set to work scrubbing the tiles until it was time to meet Will after school.

'That pie today tasted a bit weird, Mum,' said Will tentatively. 'Andy said it had liver in it.'

'Liver? It certainly didn't! It was beef!'

'He said–' Will stopped.

'What?'

'Nothing. What will tomorrow's dinner be?'

'Something nice,' I promised. 'Fishcakes and potato wedges.'

'Good,' said Will. Then, as a boy nearby called out 'Race you!' he cried, 'Wait for me, Kirk!' and sped off after him.

'It was iron beans in our day,' said the boy's mum with a grin. 'Hallo! My Kirk's new here, like your Will. You're the school cook, aren't you?'

'That's right. Still finding my feet,' I said ruefully.

'I'm sure you'll manage,' she assured me. 'It can't be as bad as the old days! When my husband Simon was a pupil here, thirty something years ago, his dinner-lady was a right old battle-axe. Apparently the kids reckoned she was trying to poison them!'

'Poison them? Really?' Startled, I wanted to know more.

But Kirk's mum was already walking away. 'See you tomorrow,' she said as she departed.

I had a question for her. Several questions. Next morning I looked for her at the school gate, but without success. So instead I took my queries to the staffroom.

'Does anyone remember the school cook from thirty or forty years ago?'

The oldest teaching assistant, Anne, looked up.

'Do you mean Mrs Pike? My goodness, she was a terror!'

'What do you mean?'

'She ruled that dining room with a rod of iron. I remember she had a thing about liver – she seemed to serve it up for every other meal. If it wasn't liver it was some awful smelly fish. She made the children clear their plates, though!'

'What happened to her?'

Anne shrugged. 'She left soon after I started, very suddenly. I don't know why.'

Could she really have tried to poison the pupils? It seemed improbable. She certainly couldn't have liked them though, I thought. Maybe there were too many complaints about the meals, and she got the sack.

And that lunchtime, seeing plates full of rejected food, I felt a surge of fear in case I went the same way.

My lovely fishcakes had disintegrated. My tasty wedges had exploded into charcoaled crumbs.

As for the peas – well, at least I could claim that they were meant to be mushy. But I'd be lucky if Mrs Mushy Peas was the worst the kids were calling me after this.

The headmistress had joined the children for dinner. Now she came over to me.

'What kind of fish was in those fishcakes, Cherry?' she asked.

'Haddock.'

'Really? They tasted... unusual. How are you finding the kitchen?'

'Very well equipped,' I said, 'but the ovens seem a bit wayward.'

'That shouldn't affect the taste, surely? The thing is, Cherry,' she said, 'several children have already asked to switch to packed lunches.'

'The dinners will improve,' I said desperately.

'I'm sure they will. Let's see how it goes next week,' she told me kindly.

I retreated to clear the plates away. There were lots of leftovers on them. Tasting some, I recoiled and pulled a face. My haddock had been fresh. Where had that rank fishy flavour come from?

The smell of it pervaded the kitchen now too. I spent an hour cleaning out fridges. While I was busy scrubbing, I heard a faint clatter in the storeroom.

'Lorna? Is that you?' Entering the storeroom, I found no sign of Lorna – but a giant pack of dried pasta had fallen from a shelf and split open. Pasta quills lay scattered all over the floor.

'That's all I need,' I muttered, reaching for the broom.

The next week, I paid extra attention to preparing the school dinners. I pulled out all the stops – in vain.

'I don't understand!' I groaned to Lorna. 'How can spicy chicken taste of liver?'

My savoury rice had turned into rice pudding – while the stewed pears were now pear gloop. Everything was overcooked.

It wasn't a one-off. That week, every meat dish that I tried to make tasted strangely and horribly of liver.

And any fish I served up had a tinge of
mackerel. I sat in the kitchen nursing a
cup of tea and feeling angry and depressed.
I knew I was a better cook than this.

Could Lorna be sabotaging my efforts?
I didn't want to believe that. Even so,
I'd started watching her – and she'd done
nothing to arouse any suspicions.

Had children been sneaking in unseen?
At first I'd thought it was a possibility.
I'd heard strange noises on a few occasions;
yet I'd never seen anyone. So I'd taken
to keeping the kitchen door locked.
And that hadn't stopped it...

I didn't like the conclusion I was coming to.
Drawing a deep breath, I went over to the
shelf where Mrs Pike's book lay.

I opened it again. Inside the front cover
was a list:

Beef liver. Mackerel. Eggs. Sardines. The entries ended abruptly in November 1988 – in mid-term. She must have got the sack then.

I'm not a superstitious person. But gazing at that spiky handwriting, I felt the hair rise on my scalp.

Behind me was a sound like a whisper. I whirled round.

I saw my freshly-cleaned counter-tops – now with salt spilt all across them. The upturned salt-pot rolled slowly in a wide circle before coming to a stop.

I stared at it. Then I spoke, my voice cracking. 'Why are you doing this? Why?'

In answer, a thin breeze sent salt pattering across the floor. And for a split second I imagined a burly woman with her sleeves rolled up, glaring at me across the counter.

The image was so vivid that I flinched.

When I blinked and looked again, I saw nothing – but I **knew**. Mrs Pike was jealous of me for taking over the kitchen where she had ruled: for trying to succeed where she had failed, over thirty years ago.

And now she would make sure that I failed too.

She didn't care about the children; she just wanted me out. She'd succeeded – for the moment, anyway. I jumped up and dashed out of the kitchen into the corridor. I had to get away from there.

As I hurried past a group of children, I heard one say loudly, 'There goes Mrs Mush!'

Wincing at the words, I took a deep breath and went into the school office where the secretary sat typing, surrounded by files.

'Jean, do you have any information about the school cook who worked here back in the nineteen-eighties?' I asked.

She looked surprised. 'My goodness! That's way before my time. I doubt it. All we've got is the old school log book.' Rummaging in a cupboard, she found a thick ledger and passed it over.

I sat in the school library to leaf through the book. It listed minor events – a special assembly, a child twisting her ankle in the playground, a trip to the zoo. The word 'hospital' caught my eye: I stopped to read more carefully – but it was just a child coming out of hospital. No mass food poisoning by the school cook.

Then I turned the page and saw her name. 'Mrs. Pike left today to care for mother after stroke. Agency cook for remainder of term.'

So maybe she wasn't sacked after all,
unless the sick mother was just an excuse...
Either way, it didn't change anything.
It didn't solve my dilemma.

The school day was ending. Deep in thought,
I went to collect Will.

Will was quiet and thoughtful too.
'Is everything okay?' I asked him.

'Yes,' he said, but I heard more children
around us murmuring: 'There's Mrs Mush!'

There and then, I vowed that somehow
I would get the better of Mrs Pike – both
for Will's sake and my own.

After an evening spent baking, I arrived at
school next day with trays of cherry flapjack.
Mrs Pike couldn't ruin those – I hoped.
As I walked across the car park, I saw Kirk
climbing out of a nearby car.

'Hi, Kirk!' I called. But he ran off, pretending not to see me. And then I realised he was trying to hide his lunchbox from my sight.

I turned to the man standing by the car.

'Are you Kirk's dad, Simon?' I asked, though I hardly needed to inquire – the resemblance between him and Kirk was very strong.
'I'm Will's Mum,' I said. 'Your wife told me that you used to come to this school.'

'That's right.' He smiled in a friendly enough way, so I went on.

'Do you remember Mrs Pike, the school cook back then?'

His eyes widened in mock alarm. 'How could I forget her? I lived in fear of her! Standing over me while I ate up all my dinner.'

'She sounds like a bully,' I said.

'Well – she was certainly formidable. She had a will of steel.'

'I'll bet,' I muttered.

'But she was only trying to help.'

'Help?'

'I was sick, you see,' said Simon. 'I had childhood leukaemia. The treatment was pretty intensive. When I got out of hospital I was still having chemo and I had real trouble eating. Mrs Pike made mushy meals specially. And then made sure I ate them.'

'What, she made them just for you?'

He laughed. 'Well, no – for everybody, so that I wouldn't feel different! Low salt, no pasta because she thought I couldn't digest it. And because I had to have plenty of Vitamin D she used to feed us the strangest things–'

'Don't tell me,' I said. 'Liver. And mackerel.'

'That's right! How did you know?'

I didn't answer that. I had an idea.
'Could you give me a hand carrying these
trays in?' I asked him.

'Sure.' Inside the kitchen, Simon set down
his tray of flapjack and gazed around.
'Memories!' he exclaimed. 'It even smells
the same. I can almost see Mrs Pike,
brandishing her ladle.'

So could I. 'Have you been back here since
those days?'

'No. When I started bringing Kirk here
three weeks ago, it was the first time I'd
been back since I left for High School.'

I reflected that that was exactly when all
the problems in the kitchen started too...

'Are you well now, Simon?' I asked. 'You recovered fully from the leukaemia?'

'Oh, yes. I was lucky – the treatment worked.'

'And of course you had Mrs Pike looking after you.'

Simon grinned. 'I'm sure that helped as well!'

'But you don't need to eat liver and mackerel these days?'

'No, thank goodness!' He headed for the door.

'Thanks,' I called after him. Then I turned to address the silent kitchen.

'You heard him,' I said. 'You saw him. He's well. And so is his son Kirk. Kirk might look just like his dad, but he's not ill.' The kitchen seemed to be listening.

'They're both perfectly well. Your meals helped Simon to recover, Mrs Pike, and he's grateful – but they're not needed any more.'

Something shifted in the air. A breeze rippled through the kitchen, and left a faint scent hanging in the air; not of fish and liver, but of scones and apples.

I got to work. While I peeled and chopped, I didn't mind the rustles round me. Mrs Pike was welcome to stay. I knew I was a good cook, and I wanted to show her that I cared for those children just as much as she had.

My shepherd's pie today would have no taste of liver. I hoped that the hungry children would empty every single plate. No more Mrs Mush; with luck, I'd be Mrs Cherry Flapjack from now on.

And guess what? I was right.

A Lock of Red Hair

'Last box!' announced Alice cheerfully, as she plonked it down on the carpet in Ben's flat.

'Let me help you unpack it,' offered Ben. He could still hardly believe that Alice was moving in with him. It was a dream come true.

He knew that Alice was the only one for him. He'd never felt this way about anyone else – and it had seemed like a miracle when Alice said she felt the same.

'Do you mind if I put a family photo here on the bookshelf?' she asked. 'It'll make me feel more at home.'

'No problem.' Ben began to unload her cardboard box.

As he pulled out a sweater, a flowery keepsake tin fell out with it and emptied its contents onto the floor.

He picked them up: a china mouse, a small wooden elephant, some shells – and a lock of short red hair tied with a black ribbon.

He held it up. 'What's this?'

'Oh, it's just – just an old memento of – of someone in the family.'

'Who?'

'Oh, nobody really.' Alice, looking embarrassed, changed the subject.

Ben glanced over at the family photo she had placed on the bookshelf; there were no obvious red-heads to be seen in it. With a shrug, he replaced the curl of hair inside the tin.

He handed it to Alice, who put it quickly in her bag. As she began to chatter about local coffee shops, he forgot about the lock of hair...

Until he cleared out a bedroom cupboard, to give Alice more room for her clothes. Right at the back, hidden behind some of her T-shirts, he found the keepsake tin.

Ben took it out and opened it. He gazed at the lock of red hair, wondering, before he carefully closed the tin and put it back. This time he didn't ask her any questions.

But after that, he noticed that Alice would often pause by her photo. Sometimes she would gently touch it with a lingering hand.

When she wasn't around, he carefully studied the picture. It was just a standard family photo.

A large group stood in a garden, with children and dogs milling around, and a radiant teenage Alice. He peered more closely at her hands. One of them rested on a dog's head – but where was the other?

Was it holding the hand of the tall boy standing close beside her? His hair looked more brown than red, but the old photo was a bit faded.

Ben knew the tall youth wasn't Alice's brother. A cousin, maybe? He reflected ruefully that Alice had never asked **him** for a keepsake lock of hair.

He tried to put it from his mind. Alice must have had admirers before him – many of them! She was such a wonderful girl that he shouldn't be surprised.

But he fretted about that lock of hair.

And suddenly their little town seemed full of red-haired men. Where did they all come from? thought Ben, dismayed.

Every time he spotted a red head, he started speculating. There was so much about Alice that he didn't know. Why was she so secretive about the lock of hair?

Maybe there was a first love that she'd never forgotten. Maybe the red lock held some hidden heartache.

Ben's own heart was aching – but he resolved not to pry. If Alice wanted to tell him, she would.

But she said nothing. Meanwhile the question ate away at him. It shouldn't have mattered, but it did.

One night, when she came in from work, Alice produced a bottle of sparkling wine.

'To celebrate our first month here together!' she announced.

'Excellent!' Ben dutifully found glasses and filled them, but he was brooding.

'Here's to my one and only!' Alice laughed, as they clinked glasses together.

He couldn't help himself. The words just slipped out.

'I'm not your one and only, though. I wasn't your first love, was I, Alice?'

She looked stunned. 'What do you mean?'

Ben took a deep breath. 'I mean a lock of red hair. Who did it belong to, Alice?'

She turned and walked over to the photo.

'Seth,' she said quietly, not looking at him.

'He's in this picture, standing next to me.'

'Seth,' repeated Ben, feeling the bottom drop out of his world. He swallowed, and said with an effort, 'I'd be happy for you to tell me about him, Alice.'

She sighed. 'I was fifteen in that photo. He was sixteen. It's true – I loved him. When he went, it broke my heart.'

Ben felt as if his heart was shattered too. He wasn't her first love at all...

Then he chided himself sternly. This is what love is. Accept it! This is part of Alice.

So, walking up to her, he squeezed her hand and said, 'I can see how much he meant to you. How important he was.'

She gave him a wistful smile.

'Oh, Ben! I didn't want to tell you.
I was afraid you might think it was really
weird, my keeping that lock of his hair.
But I'll never forget Seth. He was so lovely.'

Despite his aching heart, Ben put an arm
around Alice's shoulders and hugged her.
He might not be her first, most precious,
love; but he had to be here for her now.

'Poor Seth,' she sighed. 'Mind you,
sixteen's a good age for a dog.'

And staring at the photo, Ben fell instantly
in love again – not only with the youthful
Alice, but with the placid old red setter
by her side.

* * *

*

Printed in Great Britain
by Amazon

40352270R00090